THE LITTLE TURTLE'S BIG ADVENTURE

THE MYSTERIOUS SPARK

Hi there, everyone! I'm Tommy, and guess what? People say I'm the most curious baby turtle ever!

I live among the wiggly corals, where the colors are like a magical underwater rainbow. Every day is like a new adventure, and my little flippers can't wait to find out what's hiding beneath the waves.

With my cool family by my side, life in the depths is a daily adventure. We zip through the azure waters, playing hide-and-seek among the corals' twists and turns.

The ocean is like a giant playground, and I'm always eager to make the next amazing discovery beneath the waves, driven by my inexhaustible curiosity.

One day, my parents gathered around, cautioning me about the vast ocean's mysteries. 'Tommy,' they said, 'stay close to us. The ocean is big and mysterious, and you'll be safer with your family.'

I LISTENED CAREFULLY, UNDERSTANDING THEIR CONCERN.

WHILE PLAYING NEAR THE CORALS, A MYSTERIOUS SPARK CAUGHT MY EYE. IT TWINKLED LIKE A SECRET JUST FOR ME. UNABLE TO RESIST, I LOOKED AWAY FROM MY FAMILY. SOMETHING SPECIAL WAS WAITING, AND MY CURIOUS HEART PULLED ME CLOSER AND CLOSER.

THE COLORS AROUND IT WERE ENCHANTING, AND I COULDN'T HELP BUT FOLLOW. GETTING EVEN CLOSER, I SWAM, LEAVING THE SAFETY OF FAMILIAR WATERS BEHIND. THE UNDERWATER WORLD SEEMED TO HOLD ITS BREATH, WONDERING WHERE MY CURIOSITY WOULD TAKE ME NEXT.

As I ventured toward the mysterious spark, I entered a different part of the ocean. Here, the colors changed, and everything seemed to shimmer with an even more magical glow. I was captivated, my little heart beating with excitement.

THE OCEAN EMBRACED AN ENCHANTING DARKNESS. MY CURIOSITY AND EXCITEMENT WERE TEMPERED WITH A BIT OF NERVOUSNESS. THE DARKER IT GOT, THE MORE I WANTED TO UNCOVER THE SECRETS HIDDEN IN THE DEPTHS OF THE UNDERWATER WORLD.

As I swam through the deepening darkness, my eyes got wide with amazement. Suddenly, out of the shadows, I found an old ship, resting on the ocean floor. It looked like a big castle. I was super excited and just had to explore it!

THE OLD SHIP LOOKED SUPER COOL, I JUST HAD TO GET CLOSER! WITH EACH FLIP OF MY LITTLE FLIPPERS, I SWAM TOWARDS IT. IT FELT LIKE FINDING A GIANT UNDERWATER PLAYGROUND, AND I COULDN'T WAIT TO SEE WHAT SECRETS IT HAD HIDDEN INSIDE.

It felt like stepping into a secret world of wonders! Every room had something amazing. I peeked into corners and found old vases, bottles, and other ship stuff. It felt like the ship was telling me its story through every object, and I couldn't wait to learn more.

I FOUND SHINY SEASHELLS THAT WHISPERED TALES OF THE SEA. AS I SWAM FURTHER, COLORFUL LINES ON MAPS GUIDED ME TO MORE DISCOVERIES. MY FLIPPERS COULDN'T STOP EXPLORING! IT WAS LIKE A MAGICAL GAME OF HIDE-AND-SEEK, BUT INSTEAD OF HIDING, THE SHIP WAS SHARING ITS TREASURES.

As I continued exploring, my curiosity led me to every little corner. Suddenly, my wide eyes spotted something moving! I swam closer, wondering what it could be.

THE OCEAN FLOOR CAME ALIVE WITH A LITTLE CREATURE—AN OCTOPUS! IT SWAM GRACEFULLY, AS IF DANCING TO ITS UNDERWATER MELODY, I COULDN'T HELP BUT BE AMAZED.

When the octopus noticed me, I got a little scared. Turns out the octopus felt the same way! We both froze, like statues in water. My big eyes met the octopus's big, curious ones. As we stood still, I noticed something – we were both a little scared!

We were not moving an inch. The ship watched, the corals swayed, and the ocean held its breath, waiting to see if we could figure out how to calm our frightened hearts.

BOTH OF US, LIKE UNDERWATER NINJAS, RAN TO HIDE. I CHOSE A COZY CORNER OF THE ROOM, WHILE THE OCTOPUS FOUND HIS SECRET SPOT. WE STARED AT EACH OTHER WITHOUT SAYING A WORD.

THE SILENCE CONTINUED FOR A FEW MOMENTS, EACH CURIOUS ABOUT THE OTHER'S NEXT MOVES.

As we looked at each other, curiosity won out over fear.

I said 'Hello!' to the octopus and it replied with a friendly wave of its tentacles.

'What are you doing here?'

'Oh, hello, I'm Oliver, I live here on the ship. What about you?' said the octopus. 'I followed a spark and landed here. That was a great adventure,' I continued with a broad smile. 'And why do you live on the ship?' I finally asked, eager to hear Oliver's story.

'WELL, THE SHIP HAS BEEN HERE FOR A VERY LONG TIME. IT USED TO BE PART OF A TREASURE HUNT, BUT IT GOT CAUGHT IN A BIG STORM AND ENDED UP HERE. I'VE BEEN LOOKING AFTER IT EVER SINCE,' OLIVER REPLIED. 'WOW, THAT'S INCREDIBLE!' I SMILED. 'CAN YOU TELL ME MORE ABOUT IT?'

'WELL, BUDDY, THIS OLD SHIP HAS A TALE AS DEEP AS THE OCEAN ITSELF. IT USED TO BE ON A GRAND TREASURE HUNT, CHASING HIDDEN TREASURES FAR AND WIDE. BUT ONE NIGHT, OH BOY, ONE STORMY NIGHT, THE BIGGEST WAVE YOU CAN IMAGINE CAME CRASHING DOWN.'

The ocean roared, waves crashed, and the ship became entangled in a giant, swirling wave. The water tossed and turned, and the ship, with all its stories and treasures, ended up here at the quiet bottom of the ocean.

'I was right there, Tommy, in the midst of the roars and crashes. The ship became my home and I promised to be its guardian, keeping it safe from the secrets the ocean tries to whisper.'

I LISTENED CAREFULLY, BUT SUDDENLY, A SHIMMERING SPARK CAUGHT MY EYE, AND THE OCEAN SEEMED TO HOLD ITS BREATH. 'OLIVER, DO YOU SEE THAT SPARK? IT'S THE SAME ONE THAT LED ME HERE!' I ASKED.

'Ah, that magical spark holds a mysterious secret.'

The spark led us to a hidden corner of the ship, where a big treasure box awaited.

'What's inside, Oliver?' I whispered, holding my breath. 'Behold, Tommy! This treasure box holds gold, pearls, books, and maps—the ship's most prized possessions.' My eyes sparkled with excitement as Oliver opened the treasure chest.

'Wow!
This is incredible! I never imagined such treasures could be hidden beneath the waves.'
I replied fascinated. 'The ocean is full of surprises. Tommy.' Oliver said.

"Oliver, thank you for sharing this incredible adventure with me!' I said full of gratitude
'It was my pleasure, Tommy. I'm glad we could explore the mysteries of the deep together.'
Oliver replied with a smile.

I and Oliver exchanged smiles, feeling the warmth of our newfound friendship.

'I promise to visit you again, Oliver.' I promised.

'I'll be waiting, Tommy. Until our flippers cross paths once more, my friend.' Oliver said.

As I swam away, the ocean waves whispered tales of friendship, echoing through the deep blue sea. 'Goodbye, Oliver! I'll bring more stories next time.' I happily said.

'Goodbye, Tommy! Until our next adventure in the heart of the ocean's mysteries.' Oliver waved. I looked back, my heart was filled with gratitude for the ocean's wonders and the friend I found.

As I swam back towards my family and friends. I couldn't wait to share the tales of my underwater journey.

'You can't believe what I discovered today!'
I told them with enthusiasm as soon as I saw them.

Made in the USA
Monee, IL
27 September 2024